Along Came Grumpy

by Margaret I. Pascuzzo

Published by:

FriesenPress

Suite 300 – 852 Fort Street
Victoria, BC, Canada V8W 1H8

www.friesenpress.com

Distributed to the trade by The Ingram Book Company

Dedicated to Dr. Cher B. who inspired me to write this story.

Enjoy!
Margaret

"Help! Help!" cried Dudley, but his voice could not be heard above the excitement of the children's chatter and laughter as they bounced high on the trampoline.

"This is fun, Miliana," said Becky with a chuckle as she leapt in the air. "I'm so happy you invited me to your birthday party."

"Thank you for coming," answered Miliana. "Everyone was able to come except Geordie. He plays soccer on Saturdays and he had a game today. He did send a gift, which was kind of him," she added.

"Ouch!" groaned Dudley as the net cut into his neck. His head and two of his four wings were stuck and no matter what he did he could not free himself. It's hopeless, he thought.

The children had donned party hats and were having a wonderful time. Some played games, others bounced on the trampoline.

"Climb on the trampoline, everyone," called Krysta beckoning to the rest of the children. "Bring your noisemakers, and let's join hands in a circle around Miliana and sing Happy Birthday to her," she invited.

"Let's go, Chantel and Josh," she called to the two children standing by the table admiring a large birthday cake decorated with pink and blue icing. "The others are ready to bounce high and sing loud," she added.

Chantel and Josh quickly took their places beside the others. Miliana stood tall in the centre of the trampoline and the rest of the children formed a circle around her.

Soon the sound of horns, bells and whistles rang throughout the neighbourhood. Up in the air they went, singing at the top of their lungs.

Dudley struggled, but it was no use. His head and wings were trapped between the safety net and the trampoline. He was doomed. His thoughts turned to his family and friends. A tear fell. He dreamt of the thrill of teasing a mosquito in mid-air and wondered if he'd ever experience that same feeling again. He was deep in thought when, out of nowhere, came a mean, gruff voice.

"Be quiet out there or I'll call the police! I'm trying to sleep!" it yelled, freezing the children where they stood.

Dudley's big, bulging eyes captured a large burly man standing in the doorway of the house next door. His face was pink with rage under a thatch of gray hair. His fist was shaking high in the air. A thin, wisp of a woman with a nervous twitch to her nose stood behind him. The sad faces of the children told Dudley that this man was serious.

"Who's that?" asked Mark.

"That's our neighbour Mr. Gundy. He's so cranky all the time that the kids in the neighbourhood call him Mr. Grumpy. He doesn't like children and complains when they step on his lawn or play in the street outside his house. He never smiles. I don't like him, but Mom says I must respect him as he's old and may be sick. Even his dog, Patches, looks sad and walks with his tail between his legs. Mr. Gundy yells at him and he hides in the bushes," said Miliana.

"Poor dog," answered Mark sympathizing with Patches.

"He loves it when I pat his head or stroke his chin. He wags his tail and smiles at me," Miliana said with a grin.

"Ouch! Ouch!" muttered Dudley as each child jumped down from the trampoline.

No joyful sounds rang out as the children gazed at each other in silence. They sat at the table and ate cake and ice cream whispering and nodding to one another trying hard not to disturb Mr. Gundy. Party hats sat still on their heads. Even the happy-face balloons looked unhappy as they floated above each child's chair. The children were aware of Mr. Gundy as he lurked in his kitchen window just waiting for an opportunity to completely spoil their fun.

Dudley fretted. His bright blue body shone in the hot sun. His pink and green wings twisted in the net. I'll try to catch someone's attention one more time, he thought. Thanks to Grumpy the neighbourhood was silent. His energy was almost gone, but he did take a deep breath and called out in as loud a voice as he could.

"Help me! Help me, please!" he pleaded as the net cut into his hot, swollen body. He was sure one wing was ready to fall off. If he lost a wing he'd never be able to hover or fly backwards again. His eyes filled with tears.

"What was that?" said Thomas. "I heard a noise. It sounded like a cry for help."

Turning to his friends he asked if anyone else had heard it.

"I heard something," said Becky. "It was faint and sounded like it came from over there," she added pointing to the trampoline.

"Let's look," suggested Josh as the others got up and followed him in the general direction of the cries.

"Help, I'm over here!" spluttered Dudley. "Over here!"

The children chatted as they searched for the source of the cries. They yelled back and forth and forgot all about Mr. Gundy. They were on a mission to find whoever or whatever was crying for help.

Dudley had almost given up hope of being found when an excited voice rang out.

"Look everyone," cried Miliana pointing to the injured Dudley. "I think the cries came from this insect. It looks like he's trapped between the net and the trampoline."

"What are we going to do?" asked Robert.

The children were discussing the problem when a big, beefy hand landed on Robert's shoulder. The children turned to see a very annoyed Mr. Gundy.

"What's all the noise about?" he grimaced. "I thought I told you to be quiet or I'd call the police. Well, that's exactly what I'm going to do!" he yelled as he scowled at the children.

"B-b-but Mr. Gundy, please help us," pleaded Josh. "We found this insect trapped in the net. It's still alive and we were only trying to free it. We're sorry if we were noisy and disturbed you," he said. The other children nodded in agreement.

"Let me see," he snarled.

Dudley stiffened as Mr. Gundy took his glasses from his shirt pocket and moved to where Dudley was close to his face. To Dudley, Mr. Gundy looked like an old bulldog. His head was large, his hair which was once dark was now gray, and his big face was lined from too many frowns.

"Oh, forget it!" he snapped. "It's only a dragonfly and there are thousands of them around. The world won't miss one," he laughed as he turned and walked away.

Dudley blinked.

"Mr. Gundy, please help him. He's only a little insect," pleaded Josh as he tugged at the sleeve of the old man's shirt.

Suddenly, as quickly as he had turned to leave, Mr. Gundy turned himself around and faced Dudley. The children watched as he bent over the trapped dragonfly. His voice reached Dudley's ears. It was like a voice from heaven.

"Hold on, little fellow," he whispered. It was a voice the children had never heard before. "I'll have you free in a minute or two."

Dudley's heart hammered so hard, he felt it could be heard for miles around.

The children watched as Mr. Gundy's gentle and nimble fingers untangled the net from around Dudley's wings and neck. It was as if an invisible fairy godmother had swooped down and tapped Grumpy on the shoulder with her magic wand and transformed him from a mean, old man into a kind and caring person.

Moments later, Dudley soared in the air, happy that he could still fly. He hovered above the crowd and watched as the children hugged Mr. Gundy and thanked him for a job well done.

Dudley showed his gratitude by putting on a show for his new-found friends. He hovered; he flew backwards; he did a loop-the-loop and finished with the helicopter dance of happiness. The children waved as he headed over the tree tops.

The last thing Dudley saw as he glanced backwards was Mr. Gundy sitting at the table wearing a bright red party hat and enjoying cake and ice cream. Mrs. Gundy sat alongside him as proud as she could be. Patches, his tail wagging as fast as it could go, happily sat at his master's feet. Dudley could almost swear that he saw a smile beginning to form in the corners of the old man's mouth. The children were grateful for what Mr. Gundy had done, but none was as grateful as one dragonfly that was so happy Grumpy had come along.

About the Author

Margaret I. Pascuzzo is the author of eleven children's picture books. She was born in Glasgow, Scotland and realized at a very early age that she wanted to write for children. She worked as a Student Support Worker for many years and it was during that time that her passion became a reality. Her first book was published in December 2007 and since then her creative juices have continued to flow. Each story carries a message and is written in a way a child can understand. Her collection of warm and fuzzy stories would be an asset to any child's library.

The following books have gained recognition: "Anton Makes a Wish" "A Sad Day in the Desert" - both were runners-up in Fiction Clay Battye 2009 Contest in Penticton, B.C. and are published in the 2009 Anthology entitled "Mining for Crystal Gems" "Anton Finds a Treasure" received an Honorable Mention in the Hamilton, Ohio Writers Guild 2009 Fiction Contest.

CPSIA information can be obtained
at www.ICGtesting.com
Printed in the USA
LVIW010659210712
290880LV00002B